RESCUES
The Lonely Pony

Paula Harrison
illustrated by Olivia Chin Mueller

Feiwel and Friends · New York

For Brian and Stephanie: Thanks for all the roast dinners and scrumptious desserts

A FEIWEL AND FRIENDS BOOK
An imprint of Macmillan Publishing Group, LLC
120 Broadway, New York, NY 10271

Library of Congress Control Number: 2020911158

ISBN 978-1-250-77037-0 (hardcover)
1 3 5 7 9 10 8 6 4 2

ISBN 978-1-250-25929-5 (trade paperback)
1 3 5 7 9 10 8 6 4 2

Book design by Nosy Crow and Cindy De la Cruz
Feiwel and Friends logo designed by Filomena Tuosto

First published in the UK by Nosy Crow
as *Princess of Pets: The Lonely Pony* in 2020.
mackids.com

Chapter One
The Pony
on the Shore

Bea skipped along Savara Beach,
loving the warmth of the golden sand
beneath her toes. In the distance a
fishing boat was gliding across the
sea. The water glittered as the wind
whipped up little white-foamed waves.
Seagulls circled over the cliffs, calling
loudly. Bea began to run toward the
ocean, the sea breeze lifting her dark,
curly hair.

"Wait for me!" Her brother, Alfie, chased after her.

"Princess Beatrice! Prince Alfred!" called Nancy. "I'll be sitting over here. Make sure you keep out of the waves. If your clothes get wet, Mrs. Stickler will be upset with all of us." The palace maid settled down on a picnic blanket at the top of the beach. She folded her hands over her apron and gave a contented sigh. The palm trees that lined the seafront waved gently behind her.

Bea didn't see the point of coming to the seaside without getting wet. She jumped into a sandy rock pool, and salt water splashed all over her shorts and T-shirt. It was a lovely hot day, and she was sure her clothes would dry quickly. Mrs. Stickler, the bossy royal housekeeper, would never find out.

Alfie and Bea lived at Ruby Palace with their father, King George, and their older sister, Natasha. The palace, with its beautiful golden towers, sat high on the top of the hill outside the village. It had an enormous garden, with stables for the royal horses and an orchard full of lemon and plum trees.

Even though it was summer, King George was still busy with important royal matters, so Bea, Natasha, and Alfie had lots of time to do what they liked. Natasha, who wanted to become the best pianist in the Kingdom of Neravia, had been playing the piano for most of the morning. Alfie had been making a mud concoction in a corner of the vegetable plot.

Bea had spent the morning climbing trees with Tiger, the beautiful striped orange kitten that roamed the palace garden. Tiger loved climbing, but he was much better at going up than down. Sometimes he would get stuck at the top of a tree. Then he would meow pitifully, his furry face peering out between the branches, until Bea carried him down again.

After rescuing Tiger three times, Bea had begun teaching the little cat how to climb down by himself. It had been a fun morning, but after lunch Mrs. Stickler had sent her indoors.

"I really cannot start preparing for the Royal Garden Party with you jumping about the place, Princess Beatrice," the housekeeper had said. "I have a million things to do before all the guests arrive tomorrow, so please go inside and let me get started."

Bea went in reluctantly. The Royal Garden Party only happened once a year, and it was always lots of fun. The king had invited everyone in the village to come and be part of the special occasion. There would be games and a wonderful spread of food, and prizes for those people who'd done something to help others during the year.

Bea had wanted to help get everything ready, but Mrs. Stickler wore such a grumpy look that she didn't want to ask. She'd persuaded Nancy to take her and Alfie to the beach instead, and they had hurried out the royal gate before Mrs. Stickler could protest.

Shading her eyes, Bea looked around the beach eagerly. Sometimes she would meet her best friend, Keira, down here. Keira's gorgeous puppy, Rosie, liked running around on the sand and barking at the waves. Bea loved all animals, but she was especially fond of Rosie. She'd found the little dog lost in the palace garden a few months ago. Rosie had needed lots of careful looking after, and Bea thought she was the sweetest puppy in the world!

Bea really wanted a pet of her own, but every time she begged her dad for a hamster or a dog, or even a tortoise, he would shake his head. "Beatrice, the palace is no place for a pet," he would tell her, explaining that important guests would be shocked if there were animals running around everywhere.

Without a pet of her own, Bea had begun looking for any animals that needed her help. She had started with

Fluff, the little mouse she'd found living in a tiny hole behind the piano in the dining room, and she'd also rescued a family of doves whose tree had blown down in a storm.

Rosie the puppy and Tiger the kitten were two of her latest rescues. Rosie had grown a lot bigger since Bea first found her, but she still bounded toward Bea, wagging her tail, every time they met. There was no sign of Keira or Rosie on the beach today. The place was quite empty apart from Nancy, who was dozing on the picnic blanket, and two squabbling boys, who were being marched away from the water by their mom.

Alfie found a stick and started poking about in a rock pool, moving the seaweed around. Bea followed the shoreline, looking for shells. She especially liked the round pink ones that were smooth inside. Last time she'd come to the beach, she'd gone back home with a whole pocketful.

She walked past a cluster of tall rocks where she and Alfie sometimes liked to play pirates. She was peering at the sand so hard that she didn't spot the little gray-and-white pony until she was quite close. She stopped suddenly, her heart skipping. The little horse was standing all alone beside the water, the breeze lifting its soft gray mane.

Bea looked around, expecting to see the horse's owner, but there was no one else nearby. She took a few steps closer, but the pony twitched its ears in alarm and backed away. Bea tried again, walking very slowly and holding out her hand. She had learned to approach the horses in the royal stables this way so that they didn't get nervous. The pony snuffled at Bea's hand and shook its mane.

"Hello. You're lovely, aren't you?" Bea stroked the pony's face and noticed that the animal was quite dusty and its mane was full of tangles.

The pony gave a soft whinny and nudged her shoulder gently. Bea stared all around the beach, but no one seemed to be looking for the little horse. She noticed the creature wasn't wearing a saddle or a bridle, either.

"You must belong to someone." Bea rubbed the pony's soft neck. "I wonder how you came to be here all by yourself!"

"Princess Beatrice!" called Nancy, hurrying down the beach. "What are you doing with that pony? There's no time for

messing around. Mrs. Stickler probably expected us back hours ago."

"It seems to be here all alone, so I was wondering who it belongs to," Bea explained. "Have you seen anyone looking for a pony?"

"I don't think so." Nancy stared around distractedly. "We really must get going. Mrs. Stickler will need me to set the table for dinner. Prince Alfie! We have to go now."

Alfie waved the stick covered in seaweed over his head like a flag. "But you promised us ice cream!"

"Oh dear! I'd forgotten about that." Nancy brushed sand off her skirt. "Hurry up, then! We'll buy ice cream on the way."

Alfie dashed up the beach, trailing the seaweed stick behind him.

"I'll catch up with you," Bea told the royal maid. "I'm just going to make sure the pony gets back to its owner."

"Well, don't be long! Dinner will be at five thirty," Nancy called back.

Bea gazed around the beach as Nancy and Alfie disappeared along the road to the ice cream shop. The two boys she'd spotted with their mother had gone, and the only people left on the shoreline were an elderly couple walking along hand in hand. Bea walked up the beach, hoping to find more people she could ask about the pony.

To her surprise, the little horse trotted after her and nibbled at her hair.

"That tickles!" Bea said, laughing. "You're very friendly, aren't you?"

The pony whinnied and tossed its

head. Then it lay down and rolled back
and forth. When it leapt up again, it was
covered in sand.

"That's what I'll call you—Sandy!"
Bea smiled. "It suits you."
The pony swished her tail and blew

in Bea's ear. When Bea looked around the beach again, the elderly couple had left and the seafront was empty. The sun was turning a fiery orange as it sank toward the sparkling sea.

Bea stroked the pony's velvet coat, desperately trying to decide what to do. How had the pony come to be here all by herself? She couldn't leave the creature alone on the beach, but she really had to get back to Ruby Palace. Then an idea popped into her head.

"You can't stay here on your own after dark," she told Sandy. "You'll have to come back to the palace with me. I can look after you until I find out where you came from." She held out her hand, and the pony followed her up the beach.

Bea's heart skipped with excitement as she led Sandy along the path that took them back to Ruby Palace. There were lots of horses in the royal stables, but they were enormous creatures and Bea had to stand on tiptoe just to stroke their manes. They were mainly kept for pulling the king's carriage, which was used on special occasions.

Sandy was just the right size for Bea. She had a soft, smooth coat, and Bea loved the way the pony nibbled her hair. She couldn't wait to take Sandy back to Ruby Palace and look after her!

Chapter Two
The Hoofprints in the Garden

Bea opened the palace gate, and the pony trotted happily into the royal garden. As Bea closed the gate again, Sandy set off, cantering up the drive toward the front door as if she wanted to gallop right inside the palace.

"Sandy, wait!" Bea ran after the pony, catching her just as she reached the fountain.

Rows of tables were set out on the

grass, ready for the Royal Garden Party the next day. Chairs were lined up beside them, and there were sun umbrellas ready to offer some shade.

Bea coaxed the pony across the lawn toward the royal stables as quickly as she could. The sky was growing darker, and she knew that if she wasn't on time for dinner, she would get asked a lot of tricky questions. If she was really late, Mrs. Stickler might even come looking for her. If the housekeeper saw Sandy, she would be sure to tell King George. Then her dad would want to know why she'd brought a strange pony to the palace.

Bea would sneak Sandy into the stables for the night and then fetch her early the next morning before the grooms were up. Then they'd return to the beach to look for the pony's owner.

"Here we are, Sandy!" Bea led the pony across the stable yard. "I'll find you a stall with some hay and water." She pushed at the stable door, but it was locked and the yard was empty.

Bea frowned. She needed to find a comfortable place for Sandy to sleep, and time was running out. "I know! You can stay in the orchard tonight."

Sandy tossed her head and whinnied softly as she followed Bea to the orchard gate. Mrs. Cherry, the royal gardener, had built a fence to keep the orchard, with all its lemon and plum trees, separate from the rest of the garden. Bea led Sandy inside and closed the gate firmly. Then she found a bucket and filled it with water. The pony would be safe here, with plenty of grass to eat.

Bea hugged the pony gently. "I wish

I didn't have to go! But I'll be back first thing in the morning. I promise."

Sandy nibbled Bea's hair before leaning down to graze the grass.

"Princess Beatrice!" Mrs. Stickler's voice rang out across the garden.

Bea jumped. "Coming, Mrs. Stickler." With one last glance at Sandy, Bea ran out of the orchard, making sure to close the gate behind her.

The housekeeper was standing at the front door. "Princess Beatrice, dinner is served and we've all been waiting for you. What on earth have you been doing? You're covered in sand."

"Sorry!" Bea brushed the sand off her T-shirt. It must have gotten there when she'd hugged the pony.

"Well, there's no time to get changed," grumbled Mrs. Stickler. "Take your sandals off—as quick as you can."

Bea meekly followed the housekeeper into the dining room. At least she'd found a safe place for Sandy to sleep, and tomorrow she would give the little pony something special for breakfast.

Bea planned to get up early and visit Sandy before anyone else was awake, but when she opened her eyes, sunlight was already streaming through the curtains. An engine rumbled, and Bea peeked outside to see a delivery van pulling up to the back door. Darou, the palace chef, came running out of the kitchen, waving his arms frantically.

Bea pulled on her jeans and a T-shirt and hurried downstairs. The kitchen was buzzing as the maids rushed to and fro carrying boxes of strawberries, cherries, and plums, and enormous tubs of different-flavored ice cream. Bea waited till no one was looking before sneaking inside and taking a handful of carrots. Then she darted out the back door into the garden, her heart racing.

She'd forgotten that the garden party was today. What if someone had already been into the orchard and found Sandy?

Mrs. Stickler was outside, wiping the party tables with a cloth. "Good morning, Princess Beatrice. What on earth are you doing with those carrots?"

Bea's mind whirled. "Um . . . Well, I'm hungry and I know that carrots are really good for you . . ." The housekeeper frowned suspiciously, so Bea took a big bite of one of the carrots.

"You need to eat a proper breakfast." Mrs. Stickler scrubbed at a dirty mark on the table. "Skipping around the garden eating carrots is more suited to rabbits than princesses!"

Mrs. Cherry came past with her wheelbarrow. "Morning, Princess Bea! Which flowers would you like for the tables, Mary? I think roses would look nice."

The two women began talking about flowers. Bea turned to go but stopped when she heard Mrs. Cherry say, "And isn't it strange about the hoofprints in the vegetable garden? Something's eaten half the cucumbers, but the grooms say all the horses were locked in their stalls last night."

Bea's heart sank. Surely the cucumber stealer couldn't be Sandy! The little pony had been shut safely in the orchard.

She slipped away and ran to the orchard gate. "Sandy?" she whispered. "I've brought you some carrots."

But there was no sign of Sandy, and

when Bea searched among the trees, she found part of the fence was newly broken. She rubbed her forehead worriedly.

Sandy must have escaped, and the palace garden was so huge that the pony could be anywhere. Bea had to find the creature before she did any more damage.

Remembering what Mrs. Cherry had said about mysterious hoofprints, Bea raced toward the vegetable plot. She was halfway across the garden when there was a loud screech. A moment later, Natasha ran outside.

"Mrs. Stickler, come quickly!" she cried.

"What's wrong, Princess Natasha? Are you hurt?" The housekeeper rushed up the steps.

"There's a cow or something outside the parlor window," Natasha said breathlessly. "It was pressing its nose right up against the glass. I only caught a glimpse of it before it disappeared."

"A cow!" exclaimed Mrs. Stickler. "I don't believe it. There can't be a cow in the garden. How would it get over the palace walls?"

"There was!" cried Natasha. "It had big eyes and a long nose with huge nostrils."

Bea raced around the side of the palace and found Sandy nibbling at the roses under the parlor window. The pony tossed her head as Bea came rushing around the corner.

Bea quickly held out a carrot. She had to get the pony out of sight. "It's all right, Sandy. Look, I brought some breakfast for you."

The pony trotted over and munched the carrot eagerly. Bea heard Natasha and Mrs. Stickler approaching, so she tried to pull Sandy into the royal maze. The little pony shook her mane and refused to move.

"Come on, Sandy!" Bea's heart pounded as she offered another carrot. "You *do* like these better than the flowers, don't you?"

Sandy pricked up her ears, and at last she followed Bea into the maze, with its tall hedge walls.

"It can't have been a cow, Natasha. I think there's a horse on the loose. It's already left hoofprints all around the place," Mrs. Stickler said irritably. "I shall speak to the grooms at once. On an important day like this, they really need to keep their animals under control."

Natasha spotted Bea at the maze entrance. "What are you doing, Bea?"

Bea stuck the carrots in her pocket. "Nothing! Just going inside for breakfast."

"Yes, get some breakfast—both of you." Mrs. Stickler shooed them up the palace steps. "When you've finished eating, I'd like your help, please. There's so much to do."

"Yes, Mrs. Stickler." Natasha tucked her hair behind her ears. "Of course we'll help."

Bea sighed as she followed her sister

inside. If Mrs. Stickler had her way, she would spend the day wiping tables and tidying the garden. All she really wanted to do was take Sandy to the beach to find her owner again.

Chapter Three
Sandy's Garden Adventure

Bea bolted down her breakfast and hurried out of the royal dining room. She hoped Sandy was still safely hidden in the maze. King George stopped her in the hall. "Morning, Beatrice! Are you excited about the party?"

"Yes, I can't wait!" said Bea truthfully.

"Good! This is an important occasion for everyone," said her father. "It's the

one day each year when we thank the
people of Savara for all the wonderful
things they do. Would you like to help
me give out the prizes later?"

"Yes, please!" Bea glanced at the
door. She really had to return to Sandy
before the pony trotted away, leaving
more hoofprints everywhere.

The king smiled. "Well, off you go,
and give Mrs. Stickler a hand. I'm sure
she needs the help."

Bea hurried outside and headed
straight for the maze. She'd almost
reached it when Natasha called after her.

"Help me with these, Bea! Mrs. Stickler
wants more chairs and tables on this side
of the garden." Natasha picked up a pile
of chairs. "There are lots of people coming
from Savara. It's quite exciting, isn't it?"

"I guess so!" Bea helped her sister

move a table. She usually loved the
Royal Garden Party. The food was
always amazing. There would be
sandwiches and sausage rolls, a fruit
salad, and some kind of special dessert.

Last year, Chef Darou had baked
five different kinds of cheesecake and
decorated them all with fresh fruit. Bea
had loved the mango one so much she'd
had seconds, but this time she hadn't
thought about the garden party at all.
She could only think about Sandy.

Natasha handed Bea a white
tablecloth. "What's wrong, Bea? You're
acting really strange today."

Bea hesitated. Natasha often thought
being the eldest meant she was in
charge. If she found out about Sandy,
she was bound to go on and on about
why there should be no pets in the palace.

Natasha looked at her sister more closely. "Bea? You haven't brought another animal inside, have you?"

"Not inside exactly . . ." Bea unfolded the tablecloth and gave it a shake.

Just then, Sandy poked her nose out the maze entrance and gave a loud whinny.

Natasha gaped. "Bea, you haven't—"

"Girls!" Mrs. Stickler came rushing over with a basket full of roses and lilies. "Could you make up flower displays for the tables? And there's some bunting to be hung from the trees."

Bea panicked and held the tablecloth up high, blocking Sandy from view. "Sorry! I'm busy with this right now ..."

"Of course we'll do the flowers!" said Natasha in a rush. "Just leave it to us."

Mrs. Stickler beamed. "Thank you, that's—" Sandy snorted loudly and the housekeeper broke off to glare at Bea. "What a horrible sneeze, Princess Beatrice. Perhaps you'd better go indoors and get a tissue."

"Yes, Mrs. Stickler." Bea tried not to giggle as Sandy snuffled behind the tablecloth.

Luckily, the housekeeper hurried away to speak to Nancy, who had appeared with a large stack of picnic plates.

"Bea, where did that pony come from?" hissed Natasha. "It's much too small to be one from the stables."

"Her name's Sandy, and she was all alone on the beach yesterday," Bea explained. "I had to bring her back here before it got dark. I'm taking her to the beach to look for her owner."

Natasha sighed. "This is even worse than when you brought home the kitten!"

Bea eyed her sister closely. At least Natasha wasn't rushing off to tell Mrs. Stickler. "I'll take her away soon; I promise. I was just about to go, but Mrs. Stickler made me do all this. You won't tell anyone, will you?"

"If you're really taking her straight back to the beach, then I don't mind." Natasha gave Bea a stern look. "But that horse has got to be gone before the garden party starts. You know how important today is to everyone. Father's been preparing his speech all morning, and Mrs. Stickler has been planning everything for weeks."

Bea nodded eagerly. "Sandy will be gone soon—I promise!"

"All right! Could you help me with the flowers and the bunting before you go?" Natasha took one end of the tablecloth, and together they spread it over the table.

Natasha cut the roses and lilies carefully, and Bea put them into vases. Then they tied the bunting to the lower branches of the trees. The green and purple flags fluttered gently in the wind.

Bea suddenly spotted the pony nibbling at some of the roses. "Sandy, no!" She rushed to save them, but the pony had chewed up every last petal. "Oops! I'd better ask Mrs. Cherry for some more flowers."

"I'll go." Natasha sighed. "You should take that animal back to the beach. Her owner could be there looking for her. For goodness' sake, take her away now before she eats everything!"

Bea turned back to find Sandy
nibbling at the bunting. "Are you
hungry, Sandy? Look what I've got!"
She pulled a carrot out of her pocket, and
the pony trotted slowly after her. But as
soon as Sandy had finished the carrot,
she stopped to graze the grass again.

Bea bit her lip. "It's going to take
ages to get to the beach if I have to
lure you there with carrots. We'd get
there so much faster if I could ride you.
Would you like that?" Her heart skipped
nervously. She had ridden a few times
on the huge royal horses, but there had
always been a groom beside her, ready
to take the reins.

Sandy tossed her head and whickered
gently. Bea drew the pony down the
slope to the stables and hid her in an
empty stall. Then she fetched some

equipment from the tack room. She had never tacked up a horse by herself before, but she'd watched the grooms do it and was sure she knew what to do.

Looping the halter over Sandy's nose, she fastened it carefully. Then she placed the saddle on the pony's back and strapped everything into place. Sandy's ears pricked up, and she swished her tail eagerly.

Last of all, Bea found a brush and tried to comb the tangles out of Sandy's beautiful mane. She longed to brush the pony's coat, too, but there wasn't time. Putting on a riding hat, she tightened the strap under her chin. Sandy shook her mane and whickered again. Bea smiled. She liked seeing the pony so excited. Leading her out of the stables, Bea climbed into the saddle and took the reins.

Her stomach did a somersault and she

took a deep breath. "All right, Sandy. Let's go!" She tapped the pony's side gently with her heels.

Sandy leapt forward with a long whinny. Bea's heart skipped as they trotted across the garden, keeping behind the trees. Riding Sandy was so much easier than riding any of the royal horses the grooms had let her try.

Natasha was waiting by the palace gate. "Go quickly!" she told Bea. "Mrs. Stickler's gone inside to look for table napkins, but she'll be back in a minute and there are maids everywhere."

"Thanks, Natasha." Bea looked at her sister in surprise.

"Don't be late." Natasha pulled the gate open. "The garden party starts at two o'clock, and I can't cover for you forever."

"I'll try not to take too long," Bea called back as Sandy dashed through the gate. She held the reins tight. The wind rushed past, and she felt like she was flying as Sandy galloped down the hill to Savara.

Chapter Four
Danger
on the Sand

Bea rode all the way into Savara on Sandy's back. She pulled on the reins as they reached the bottom of the hill, and the pony whinnied and slowed down into a walk. Bea smiled at everyone as she passed by. Mr. Patel from the bakery waved at her. "See you at the garden party, Princess Beatrice!" he called.

"Yes, see you soon!" Bea smiled,

careful not to let go of the reins in case she wobbled.

Bea guided the pony toward the seafront, where palm trees fluttered in the breeze. Excitement fizzed inside her. This felt so smooth and easy, not bumpy like riding the enormous horses from the royal stables. She gently steered Sandy onto the warm, golden sand. The sea sparkled brightly, and the wind was whipping up little silver-tipped waves.

Bea jumped down and looped the reins around her hand. Sandy snorted and shook her pale mane. The little pony seemed so much happier now than she had been the day before. Her eyes were bright and her tail swished joyfully.

"Does your owner ride you all the time?" Bea asked Sandy softly. "You must really miss them." She looked around the beach, wondering if Sandy's owner was already here.

There was a family sitting on a picnic blanket eating their lunch, and a boy and his grandma building a ring of sandcastles. None of the people paid any attention to Bea and Sandy. Bea suddenly wondered what Sandy's owner was like. Surely a good owner would have looked after the pony better and kept her safe.

Sandy whickered gently and nudged Bea's shoulder with her nose.

"Are you hungry?" Bea offered Sandy the last carrot out of her pocket, but the pony didn't take it. She whinnied and bumped Bea's shoulder a second time.

"Do you want to go riding again?" asked Bea, smiling.

Sandy's ears pricked up, so Bea climbed back into the saddle and tapped

her heels against the pony's sides. Sandy
swished her tail and cantered into

the shallows, sending up fountains of sparkling spray with her hooves.

Bea laughed and tugged on the reins as they drew closer to the cliff. Sandy wheeled around and galloped back along the sand. The wind whirled around them, and Bea felt like she was racing the fluffy clouds scudding across the sky.

Sandy and Bea cantered up and down the shore for a long time. At last Bea looked at her watch. It was already a quarter past one, and she still wasn't any closer to finding Sandy's owner. Maybe she should walk into the village and ask if anyone had been searching for a lost pony?

"Stay here, Sandy." She tied the pony's reins to a post at the top of the beach. "I'll be back really soon." She stroked

Sandy's nose, but the pony stood looking straight ahead.

Bea hurried along the street. She didn't want to leave Sandy for too long. The pony had changed as soon as Bea had tied her reins to the post. Her ears had drooped and her tail had stopped moving. Maybe she hated being tethered.

Bea went into the bakery looking for Mr. Patel. The baker was busy, and as Bea stood waiting, there was a tap on her shoulder.

"Hello, Bea!" Keira smiled. "I didn't think I'd see you till the party."

"Hi, Keira." Bea grinned. "Is Rosie with you?"

"No, my dad took her for a walk today. I've just been buying some things for the café, and now I'm going back to get ready for the garden party." Keira held up a shopping bag with some oranges and tomatoes. Keira's family, the Makalis, ran the Sleepy Gull Café on the clifftop, and Keira helped out there all the time.

"You've got to come and see my pony!" Bea said excitedly. "She's called Sandy and she's really cute."

"Did your dad let you have your own horse?" Keira's eyes widened.

"No, I found her all alone on the beach yesterday, and I'm still looking for her owner." Bea grabbed Keira's arm and pulled her to the door. "She's such a sweet pony. Come and see!"

The girls hurried back to the beach. Bea was about to point Sandy out when she noticed that the pony's head was raised and her ears were pinned back. Suddenly the little horse began pawing at the ground.

"Something's wrong!" Bea started running.

Sandy tossed her head fiercely and whinnied. A thin green shape twisted and coiled on the sand.

"There's a snake, Bea," called Keira. "Right there by her hooves."

The snake raised its pointed head into the air and flicked its tongue. Its body rippled as it slid closer to the pony's hooves.

"She must be scared of them," panted Bea. "Quick, before she panics!"

The pony rolled her eyes and pawed the ground again.

Bea recognized the snake's brown-and-green markings. She'd seen this kind of snake before on the cliff path, and she knew it wasn't venomous. "Sandy, it's just a grass snake. It can't hurt you!"

The pony backed away, snorting,
but she was tied fast to the post. The
reins drew tight, straining against
the wood. Sandy tossed her head
again, and the knot in the reins began
to loosen. Bea rushed forward, but
the knot unraveled, and, suddenly
free, the pony galloped away across
the beach.

"Sandy, wait!" called Bea. "Everything's going to be all right."

But Sandy only galloped faster. Reaching the other side of the beach, she cantered up the narrow track that led through the bushes away from Savara. Soon the little pony was lost among the trees.

Bea stopped to catch her breath. "I didn't see a snake here when I left her. I never should have tied her to that post."

"It's not your fault." Keira put an arm around her friend. "You couldn't leave her loose, either. Maybe she'll come back in a minute."

But the little pony didn't reappear. Bea's heart sank. Sandy was all alone again, and she might keep on galloping for miles. What if it was impossible to find her?

Chapter Five
Silver Gate Farm

Keira and Bea scrambled up the narrow track where Sandy had disappeared. A rabbit scuttled into its burrow as they pushed past the thick, prickly bushes. They crossed a tangled piece of scrubland scattered with wildflowers and followed a zigzagging path up the slope. The beach grew smaller behind them.

They stopped at the top to catch

their breath. The track they'd followed
joined the narrow road that led to
Ruby Palace. Bea glanced right and
left, wondering which way Sandy might
have gone. To her right, the gates of
Ruby Palace were open and gleaming
in the afternoon sunshine. The guests for
the Royal Garden Party hadn't started
arriving yet.

"Hey, these look like hoofprints."
Keira pointed to a line of round marks
on the dusty roadside.

Bea's heart leapt. "Then Sandy
definitely came down here! But which
way was she going?"

"This way, I think." Keira pointed left
to where the road led away from the
palace.

Bea peered closely at the hoofprints. "She must have been so scared by that snake that she just kept galloping."

"I hope she hasn't gotten too far." Keira peered down the lane.

Bea looked back toward the palace gate. Guests would start arriving for the garden party very soon, and she was supposed to be there, dressed in her best clothes and ready to welcome everyone. She rubbed her forehead worriedly. She just had to search for Sandy first. The little pony could be in danger.

Keira and Bea hurried along the lane, following the hoofprints. The road grew narrower until it was just a dirt track with two deep grooves worn by the wheels of passing vehicles.

"Maybe it isn't an accident that Sandy came this way," Bea said suddenly. "What if this is where she lives?"

"It would be lovely if she's found her way home," said Keira.

"I guess so." Bea ducked under some low-hanging branches at the side of the lane. If Sandy had found her way home, that *was* good . . . but what if she never saw the little pony again?

Around the next corner, the lane ended in a large gate hung with a sign that read SILVER GATE FARM. An old farmhouse stood at the far side of a dusty yard. Behind the building there were several fields of brown-and-white cows, but the nearest field had just one small cow grazing on the grass.

Bea climbed onto the gate and shaded her eyes. The cow standing all alone wasn't a cow at all. It was Sandy!

Keira spotted the pony at the exact same moment. "There she is! You were right, Bea. She must have known where she was going."

Bea took off her riding hat, Keira dropped her shopping bag on the grass, and they both scrambled over the gate.

"Sandy, are you all right?" Bea ran across the paddock.

Sandy flattened her ears and backed away. Then she tossed her head and whinnied as the girls drew closer. Bea threw her arms around the pony's neck. "I'm sorry the snake scared you!"

The pony stayed quite still, and when Bea released her, she backed away a little more.

"You've lost your saddle, too," said Bea. "You must have galloped so fast it fell off! Maybe I didn't strap it on properly."

"She must have jumped over the fence to get back in." Keira stroked the pony gently. "That's quite a big jump for such a small pony!"

"We'd better tell the people who live here that she's come home. They must have missed her." Bea gazed around the empty farmyard. She couldn't shake off the feeling that something wasn't right.

Why hadn't the farmer come out to meet them?

The girls had just begun to climb over the fence into the farmyard when a large black dog rushed out of a barn, barking wildly.

Bea stopped with one leg swung over the fence. "Hello!" she called toward the farmhouse. "Can you call off your dog? We've come to talk to you."

"It's about your pony," added Keira.

But no one appeared, and the dog began growling and jumping up at the fence.

"Maybe no one's home," said Keira. "But we can come back and talk to Sandy's owner later. At least she's safe for now."

Bea frowned. "What if this is the wrong place? I don't think I can leave

Sandy here unless I know for sure that it's her real home."

"But she jumped right over the fence into this field!" said Keira. "I thought you wanted to find her owner."

"I do!" Bea flushed. "But how do we know she belongs here without speaking to anyone? I think I should take her back to the palace."

Keira patted the pony's neck. "Don't you think you're just trying to keep the pony for yourself?"

"I'm not!" Bea shook back her dark, curly hair. "I'm trying to do the best thing for Sandy."

Keira put her hand on Bea's arm. "Don't be upset, Bea! It's just that she seems so happy here. Why don't we come and check on her after the garden party?"

Bea sighed. "I guess you're right." She checked her watch. "Uh-oh! I said I'd be back by two o'clock for the party, and it's half past two already." She gave the pony another hug. "Bye, Sandy! I promise I'll check on you later."

Sandy gave a snort and went back to grazing the grass. Keira and Bea climbed over the fence and ran down the lane. When they reached the palace gates, people were pouring into the royal garden, wearing their best clothes and sun hats. Even more people were streaming up the hill from Savara, and many of them were carrying salads and baskets of cupcakes to add to the picnic food. There was a happy buzz of chatter.

"Look, it's Princess Beatrice returning for the party," said Mr. Patel. "Make

way, everyone! Have you been off on an adventure, Princess Beatrice?"

Bea blushed as she and Keira walked inside. "We were helping a lost pony," she told him. She suddenly wondered whether Mr. Patel knew who owned Silver Gate Farm. "Do you know who lives at the farm just down the lane—the one with all the cows?"

The baker looked puzzled. "I'm not sure I know which one you mean, Princess Beatrice. Which direction was it?"

Bea was just about to explain, when Alfie dashed up to them. "I've been looking for you for ages!" he panted. "Mrs. Stickler's gone wild because she can't find you. You'd better hurry up."

Bea glanced down at her grubby jeans. The housekeeper would be even more upset once she saw the state of her clothes, and there wasn't time to sneak inside to change. Bea tried to drag her fingers through her tangled hair. How could she explain being covered in dust at the most important royal occasion of the whole year?

Chapter Six
The Trouble
with Trifle

Bea brushed hastily at her T-shirt as she made her way across the garden. Her fingers were so dirty that she didn't know if she was making things worse. King George was standing by the palace steps, smiling and shaking the guests' hands. Bea crossed her fingers that he didn't look too closely at her clothes.

"Beatrice, there you are!" King

George boomed. "Hello, Keira! Are your parents here, too?"

"They're just finishing the lunch orders at the café. They'll be here really soon," said Keira, bobbing a curtsy.

"That's excellent!" The king smiled broadly. "Why don't you girls get some food? The ham rolls are very tasty."

Bea's stomach rumbled, reminding her that she hadn't eaten any lunch yet. By the time she and Keira had made their way through the crowd to the picnic table, Mrs. Stickler had disappeared into the palace kitchen with a stack of empty plates.

Bea picked up a roll and some cucumber and carrot sticks. The carrots reminded her of Sandy, and she felt a twist of sadness. Sandy was such an adorable pony. Bea hoped whoever lived at Silver Gate Farm would look after her properly. As soon as the garden party was over, she'd go back and check on her.

"Are you all right, Bea?" said Keira, picking up a pizza slice. "Ooh, look at those flowers! I think something's chewed them."

Bea looked up quickly. The roses in each vase had been chewed almost down to the stalks. Natasha was supposed to have thrown out the flowers that Sandy had eaten and replaced them with new ones. "That's weird! I wonder . . ." She broke off as Mrs. Stickler came out of the kitchen carrying a vast dessert dish filled with the largest and most amazing trifle that Bea had ever seen.

It was a huge wobbling concoction of plum jelly and chocolate sponge cake, topped with extravagant swirls of cream. Multicolored flower sweets were scattered over the top like a bouquet. There was a gasp from the crowd followed by murmurs of admiration.

Natasha followed Mrs. Stickler with a large stack of bowls. "I decorated the top of the trifle," she told everyone proudly.

Bea edged closer to her sister, whispering, "Natasha, didn't you change the flowers after I left?"

Natasha wasn't really listening. "Watch out, Bea! I don't want to drop these."

Mrs. Stickler placed the dessert dish carefully on the table. Then she spotted Bea and frowned. "Why haven't you brushed your hair, Princess Beatrice? And what happened to the nice dress you were going to wear?"

Bea shuffled her feet. "I meant to go and get changed, but I got really busy and—" She broke off, catching sight of something over the housekeeper's shoulder.

Two ladies stood talking beside the

maze entrance. One was wearing a yellow hat decorated with large pink daisies. Bea watched as some of the flowers were whisked into the air and then disappeared behind the hedge.

"Bea!" Natasha nudged her. "Mrs. Stickler's talking to you."

"Oh, sorry!" Bea peered at the lady with the daisy hat. For a second, she thought she'd seen pony ears sticking up behind the hedge, but that was impossible! They'd left Sandy safe and sound at the farm. There was no way the pony could have trotted into the royal garden without lots of people noticing.

King George tapped his glass. "Gather round, everyone! I'd just like to say a few words before we all try out this delicious trifle."

Everyone gathered around the king.

"First of all, I'd like to thank you all for coming," the king said. "Secondly, I must thank Mrs. Stickler for all her hard work—for the food and the flower displays." Bea looked doubtfully at the vases of chewed flowers. "Thirdly, I'd like

to thank Princess Natasha and Princess
Beatrice, who helped out and . . ."

Bea became distracted by a loud
slurping noise behind her. Swinging
around, she saw Sandy beside the picnic
table, nibbling at the flower sweets on
top of the trifle. She stared at the pony.
"Sandy! How did you get here?"

Mrs. Stickler gave a loud shriek and tried to shoo the pony away, but Sandy was enjoying the plum jelly and cream too much to move. "Get away, you horrible animal! That's it—I'm fetching the grooms." She marched off toward the stables.

"What on earth is that pony doing in my garden?" exclaimed King George. "It's certainly not one of my horses."

"Bea!" Natasha hissed under her breath. "I thought you took the pony away. I told you it had to be gone before the party."

"I did take it away!" Bea hissed back.

"What's that?" The king looked at his daughters, a frown growing on his face. "Girls, do you know something about this?"

"This is Sandy, and I found her all

alone on the beach yesterday," explained
Bea. "When I couldn't find her owner,
I brought her back here for the night,
but I think she lives at a farm down the
road. I left her there just now—I really
don't know how she got back here!"

Sandy whinnied and continued
chewing on the flower sweets. Her nose
was covered with cream and jelly. The
two ladies standing by the maze shook
their heads disapprovingly. A little boy
in a red sun hat pointed at the pony and
giggled.

"Beatrice, you really must learn to
think!" said King George sternly. "Ponies
have no place at a royal garden party."

Sandy tossed her head, nervous at the
raised voices. She trotted into the crowd,
making the guests scatter left and right.
Then she gave a huge snort, covering

Natasha's dress with trifle. Natasha shrieked. Grabbing a napkin, she dabbed at the spilled cream and jelly.

Bea stared in horror at the streaks of

purple and white across her sister's dress. "Sandy! Come here." She took hold of the pony and tried to lead her away. "I'm really sorry, everyone!"

Mrs. Stickler returned with two grooms and ordered them to take Sandy to the stables. "I've called Stray Animal Services, and they'll be here in half an hour," she informed the king. "They're bringing a horse trailer to take the animal away."

King George nodded approvingly. The grooms took hold of Sandy's reins and led her toward the stables.

Bea swallowed. Sandy would be taken away in half an hour! After that she'd probably never see the little pony again.

"And Princess Beatrice," added Mrs. Stickler, "we're going to need a lot more napkins to clean up this mess. Please fetch them for me."

"Yes, Mrs. Stickler." Bea turned to her father. "But, Dad! Can't we keep Sandy for a little while longer? She's a great pony, and she loves being ridden."

"That's enough, Beatrice!" King George's face darkened like a thundercloud. "I'm very disappointed that you didn't care about our garden party. There will be no more unexpected animals brought into Ruby Palace. Now do as Mrs. Stickler asks at once."

Bea's cheeks turned scarlet as she hurried away. She had never seen her dad look so annoyed before. If he didn't forgive her for bringing Sandy to Ruby Palace, this could be the end of her helping animals forever.

Chapter Seven
A Pony Surprise

Bea grabbed the napkins from inside and mopped up the spilled trifle on the picnic table. When she tried to follow the grooms taking Sandy to the stables, Mrs. Stickler stopped her. "No, Princess Beatrice. Let the grooms deal with this now, please."

The housekeeper rushed off to help Natasha find another dress to wear. Tears pricked Bea's eyes.

"Bea!" Keira grabbed her arm. "I've just realized I left my bags by the farm gate. I put them down before we climbed over the fence to see Sandy and accidentally left them there. Will you help me fetch them?"

Bea nodded, grateful to her friend for giving her a reason to leave the party and escape all the disapproving glances. Maybe by the time she got back, everyone would have calmed down. As she trailed out the palace gate after Keira, her dad's words echoed in her ears: *Beatrice, you really must learn to think!*

Her cheeks reddened again as she thought about Sandy eating the magnificent trifle. She'd only wanted to look after the pony. How had everything gone so wrong?

"I *still* don't understand how Sandy

got into your garden," said Keira for the third time. "We left her right there in the field."

"I don't understand, either." Bea sighed. "But now my dad thinks I don't care about the garden party, and that's not true!"

They turned the corner, and the lane became a dirt track leading to the farm. Bea stopped by the farm gate to pick up Keira's shopping bag. Her riding hat was lying there, too.

"Bea—look!" Keira grabbed her friend's arm.

Bea turned around, and her stomach did a somersault.

Sandy was standing right where they'd left her. She raised her head to look at the girls, flicking her left ear.

"How did she get there?" cried Bea.

"It's like magic! One minute she's at the palace, and the next minute she's here again."

Keira shook her head. "This is really strange. Sandy should be in the stables with those grooms."

Bea hooked the shopping bag over her arm and climbed the fence into Sandy's field. The pony bent her head to graze the grass. Her soft dapple-gray coat gleamed in the summer sunshine.

Suddenly things began to fit together in Bea's head like the pieces of a jigsaw puzzle. "Do you remember that Sandy lost her saddle?" she began slowly. "And we

thought it had fallen off when she ran away from the grass snake?"

"I remember," said Keira. "Will your dad be upset that it's lost?"

Bea shook her head. "It's not that! Sandy was wearing the saddle when we saw her at the palace just now."

Keira looked puzzled. "But that makes no sense! Where has it gone?"

"I think Sandy's still wearing it— at the palace." Bea pushed back her tangled curls. "I think there are two ponies that look the same. They're probably sisters!"

"So . . . you're saying that Sandy's the one at the palace wearing the saddle, and this pony is her sister?" Keira frowned.

"I think so! When Sandy left the beach, she must have galloped straight into the palace garden before any of the

guests arrived. Then we followed the
hoofprints in the wrong direction and
ended up here . . . and when we saw this
pony, we thought it was Sandy!"

Keira nodded slowly. "That would
explain how the pony seemed to be in
two places at once! But what are we
going to do now? Mrs. Stickler's already
called Stray Animal Services, and they'll
take Sandy away."

"I know—we haven't got long."
Bea chewed her lip. "I'm going to try
knocking on the farmhouse door."

Keira nodded. "Be careful of the dog!"
The little pony trotted over and nuzzled
her shoulder. Keira smiled and rubbed
the animal's nose. "I'll stay here and
keep an eye on the pony."

Bea scrambled over the fence into the
yard, ran to the farmhouse door, and

knocked firmly. She saw Keira waving at her and quickly waved back. The door opened, and an old man with wispy gray hair peered out.

"Sorry to disturb you!" said Bea nervously. "I'm Bea and that's my friend Keira. I live at Ruby Palace."

"You're one of the princesses, aren't you?" The man scratched his head and grinned. "Well, it isn't every day that I get a royal visit!"

"I was wondering whether you'd lost a pony," continued Bea. "I found one on the beach and—"

"What's that? Have you seen my pony Bella?" The man opened the door wider. "I've been looking for her everywhere. Bunty hasn't been the same without her. I think she's pining!"

"Is Bunty the name of the other pony?"

Bea jerked back suddenly as a dog came rushing out the door, barking loudly.

"Get down, Casper!" The man took hold of the dog's collar. "Don't worry; he wouldn't hurt a fly. I'm Mr. Morley."

Bea quickly told Mr. Morley how she'd found Sandy on the beach and how she had looked after her until the little horse had been frightened by the snake and ran away. "So when we found your farm, we got mixed up and thought your other pony was Sandy," she added. "They look so similar."

"They're twins," Mr. Morley told her. "I bought them for my granddaughters to ride, but when my son got a new job, their family had to move away from Savara. Since then the ponies have been restless—especially Bella. She loves to be ridden." He gave a deep sigh. "I'd love to spend more time with them, but I have all my cows to take care of. Anyway, yesterday I left the gate ajar by mistake, and Bella disappeared."

Bea nodded. "That explains how she got loose." She took a deep breath. "Do you think my friend and I could take your other pony, Bunty, to the palace? I need to show her to my dad so that I can explain everything. The trouble is that Sandy, I mean Bella, could be taken away by Stray Animal Services any minute now!"

"You'd better hurry, then," said Mr. Morley. "I'll drive along in my van and meet you at the palace."

While Mr. Morley looked for his van keys, Bea raced back to Keira. "I was right—there are two ponies!" she panted. "This one's called Bunty, and we can take her back to the palace to explain."

"It might be too late," Keira said. "That's why I was waving at you. They were going to take Sandy away in half an hour, and that time's almost up!"

Bea stroked Bunty's nose. Her brain spun like a fairground ride. "Then I'll just have to ride back! It'll be quicker." She handed Keira the shopping bag and grabbed the riding hat that she'd left on the ground. Then she scrambled onto the pony's back.

She'd never ridden without a saddle before, and the pony's coat felt smooth and slippery. She remembered how

easy it had been riding Sandy that
morning. She knew she could do this!
She threaded her fingers through Bunty's
mane.

Bunty looked around in surprise and
whinnied happily. Keira opened the
gate leading to the lane. Bea tapped the
pony's sides gently, and Bunty jumped
forward, her tail swishing.

"I'll meet you there!" Bea called
to Keira. Then she leaned forward to
whisper into the pony's ear. "Come on,
Bunty! We're going to save your sister."

The pony whickered and broke into
a canter, her hooves thudding on the
ground. Bea's dark curls bounced on
her shoulders as they sped toward Ruby
Palace.

Chapter Eight
Bella
and Bunty

Bea's heart sank when she saw a horse trailer parked outside the palace gates. Someone from Stray Animal Services must already have arrived. Soon they would take Sandy away.

Bunty stopped outside the gates and tossed her head nervously. There was a buzz of voices from inside the royal garden.

"It's all right, Bunty!" Bea spoke

soothingly and patted the pony's neck, but Bunty still wouldn't go through the gates. "You're a bit shyer than your sister, aren't you?"

Bunty whinnied and twitched her ears. Bea gently tapped her heels against the pony's flanks, and at last Bunty walked through the gate.

"Good girl, Bunty!" Bea whispered as they trotted along the palace drive.

Most of the guests were clustered around the picnic table. Natasha spotted Bea first and she rushed over, saying, "Why have you taken that pony from the stables, Bea? You know you weren't supposed to."

Bea climbed down from the pony's back and held the reins tightly. "This isn't the same pony. This is a different one."

"Honestly! Aren't you in enough

trouble already?" Natasha rolled her eyes. "You weren't allowed to keep the first animal, so you fetch another one straightaway."

"It's not like that!" Bea stroked Bunty, who looked as if she was about to bolt. "Look, I'm really sorry about your dress—"

"What will Dad say?" interrupted Natasha. "Chef Darou had to start making a whole new trifle after what your last pony did."

Before Bea could answer, the crowd parted and King George marched through. A lady wearing a red T-shirt with STRAY ANIMAL SERVICES on it followed him, leading Sandy by the reins. The king saw Bea with Bunty and stopped in surprise. The ponies spotted each other at the same moment and neighed joyfully.

King George looked from one pony to the other. "Beatrice, what on earth . . ."

"Dad, I never meant to keep a stray pony here during the garden party. I'm really sorry about everything!" Bea felt tears prick her eyes, and she wiped them away. "It was all a mistake . . . I thought I'd left Sandy at the farm, but I'd gotten confused because there are two ponies!" She explained what had happened when Sandy got scared by the snake and ran away.

By the time she'd finished explaining, Keira and Mr. Morley had arrived. "So we got mixed up because the ponies look so alike," finished Bea.

"They're almost exactly the same." Keira looked from Sandy to Bunty. "The only difference is that Bunty's a little smaller and Sandy has larger gray spots on her back."

Mr. Morley bowed his head to the king. "Good afternoon, Your Majesty. I'm very grateful to these girls for helping me find Bella. If it wasn't for them, she might still be wandering around on the beach."

"I see!" King George wrinkled his brow. "So, you're the ponies' owner, then. And which one is Bella?"

"I've been calling her Sandy because she rolled around on the beach and got covered in sand," said Bea with a smile.

Sandy whickered and nibbled Bea's hair.

"I can see how much she likes you," Mr. Morley told Bea. "You seem to have a knack with ponies."

The king's stern face softened a little. "I think Beatrice has a knack with all animals. *That* has been part of the problem!"

"I'll always be glad that she found little Bella," said Mr. Morley. "These ponies were meant for my granddaughters to ride. They've been restless ever since the girls moved away. They just don't get ridden very much anymore."

An idea lit up Bea's mind like sunshine on a cloudy day. "What if Keira and I came to ride them? Then they wouldn't feel so restless. We could look after them, too—brush their coats and manes. I've watched the grooms taking care of the royal horses, so I think I know what to do."

King George sighed. "I'm afraid that's not possible, Beatrice. Farms are busy places, and I'm sure you'd be in the way."

"I'd be happy for them to visit, sire," said Mr. Morley. "In fact, they'd be doing me a favor. These ponies need love and care, and I have a whole herd of cows to look after. I just don't have the time!"

Bea gazed at her dad and held her breath.

"Very well," the king said at last. "You may go to the farm to ride the ponies . . . on one condition. I shall buy you some riding boots and a riding hat that fits properly, and you *must* wear them."

"Thanks, Dad!" Bea hugged him before turning to Keira. "You'll ride with me, won't you?"

Keira beamed. "I'd love to!"

Sandy nibbled the king's arm, and he brushed his sleeve hastily before turning to the lady from Stray Animal Services. "I'm sorry to have wasted your time. Would you like to stay and enjoy the party?"

The lady smiled. "Thank you, Your Majesty. I'm just glad the ponies will be back where they belong." She handed Sandy's reins to Mr. Morley.

"Excuse me!" Mrs. Stickler's voice cut through the crowd. "Make way, please." She appeared carrying a second trifle—even more splendid than the one before—with swirls of chocolate cream and fresh strawberries on top.

The trifle wobbled as the housekeeper set it carefully down on the picnic table. She scowled when she spotted Sandy and Bunty. "More ponies! Sire, is this a good idea?"

Mr. Morley, who hadn't noticed Mrs. Stickler's grim face, rubbed his hands together happily. "That pudding looks delicious! You know—my ponies are very fond of a bowlful of trifle!"

"We know!" said Bea and Keira, giggling.

The laughter spread around the crowd, and Sandy joined in with a loud whinny.

Chapter Nine
Pony Girls

Everyone had a wonderful time at the Royal Garden Party, except for Mrs. Stickler, who didn't even cheer up when Bea replaced all the nibbled flowers on the tables with fresh pink roses. The trifle was a great success, and Bea and Keira managed two bowlfuls each. Alfie ate four helpings before complaining that his stomach hurt.

Bea helped King George give out

the prizes. Mr. Patel won an award for helping his neighbors, and Mrs. Cherry was given another for growing delicious vegetables. Everyone agreed that it had been a lovely garden party—even better than the year before.

The next day, Keira arrived early at Ruby Palace. She and Bea went to the royal stables to have a lesson in pony care from the head groom, Sally. The groom had tied up Peppermint, one of the calmest horses in the stable, for them to practice on.

Bea's stomach gave a somersault as she waited for Sally to collect all the grooming equipment. She'd watched the stable hands lots of times, but she'd never had a proper lesson on looking after a pony before.

"It's important to groom ponies

carefully, especially after riding them,"
Sally told the girls. "First, use the dandy
brush to remove any mud, like this." She
showed them how to use different brushes
to groom Peppermint, before using a
damp sponge to clean around the horse's
eyes and muzzle.

"Using a hoof pick is really important."
Sally explained how to get loose stones
out of a horse's hooves. Lastly, she showed
them how to brush and braid a mane.
By the time they'd finished, Peppermint's
mane looked beautiful and her coat was
gleaming.

"You've done a wonderful job," Sally
said, nodding approvingly. "I think
you're ready to groom Mr. Morley's
ponies."

"Thanks for teaching us!" Bea grabbed
her riding hat, fizzing with excitement.

"Come on, Keira! Mr. Morley said we could visit as early as we liked."

Bea and Keira rushed down the lane to Silver Gate Farm. Mr. Morley was already out in the fields looking after the cows, and he gave the girls a cheery wave. Sandy came trotting over right away, while Bunty ducked her head shyly.

"Hello, Sandy!" Bea stroked the pony's neck and giggled when the little horse nibbled her hair. "I know you're supposed to be called Bella, but I think Sandy suits you better."

Keira gently rubbed Bunty's nose and offered her an apple that she'd brought from the café. Then she strapped on the riding hat that she'd borrowed from the royal stables. Bunty crunched the apple, her tail swishing.

The girls brushed the ponies the way Sally had showed them, before putting on the saddles and halters. Sandy's ears pricked as soon as Bea fastened her collar. She whinnied happily and stamped her feet.

"Stay still a minute, Sandy," Bea said, laughing. "I've got to make sure everything's done properly."

With her saddle strapped on, Sandy pranced over to the gate and stood there, waiting for Bea.

Keira tightened her pony's halter. "There you are, Bunty. You're ready, too."

Bea and Keira rode the ponies down the lane. Sandy stepped forward eagerly, but Bunty tossed her head and shied away when a cyclist rode past.

Keira climbed down and took hold of the reins. "Let's lead them down the hill. I don't think Bunty likes the noise and traffic."

"Good idea," said Bea, climbing down from Sandy's back.

Bunty's ears pricked up as soon as they reached the seafront. The golden sand gleamed in the bright sunshine, and the palm trees swayed in the breeze. Bea scrambled onto Sandy's back, and the pony sprang forward, whinnying.

"Wait for me!" Keira climbed onto

Bunty's back and urged the little horse forward.

Sandy reached the sea first and galloped into the shallows. Her hooves sent glittering spray flying into the air. Bunty followed and the two ponies raced across the beach together.

Bea pulled on Sandy's reins as they reached the other side. "Whoa, Sandy!"

Sandy whickered and started pulling clumps of grass from the cliff.

"Just think!" Bea leaned forward to stroke the pony's neck. "We can spend the whole summer looking after the ponies. We can ride on the beach or at the farm every day!"

"Don't forget playing with Rosie and taking care of your kitten!" said Keira, grinning. "You have lots of animals to look after now. Do you think you'll have time for any new ones?"

"Don't worry! I'll always have time for more animals," Bea said firmly.

The girls turned the ponies around and cantered back along the beach. Bea's heart skipped as Sandy sped up and her hooves thundered on the warm golden sand.

Thank you for reading this **Feiwel and Friends** book.

The Friends who made

ROYAL RESCUES
The Lonely Pony

possible are:

Jean Feiwel, Publisher

Liz Szabla, Associate Publisher

Rich Deas, Senior Creative Director

Holly West, Senior Editor

Anna Roberto, Senior Editor

Kat Brzozowski, Senior Editor

Dawn Ryan, Senior Managing Editor

Kim Waymer, Senior Production Manager

Erin Siu, Associate Editor

Emily Settle, Associate Editor

Rachel Diebel, Assistant Editor

Foyinsi Adegbonmire, Editorial Assistant

Cindy De la Cruz, Associate Designer

Avia Perez, Production Editor

Aurora Parlagreco, Senior Designer

Follow us on Facebook or visit us online at mackids.com

OUR BOOKS ARE FRIENDS FOR LIFE